Published by First Second
First Second is an imprint of Roaring Brook Press,
a division of Holtzbrinck Publishing Holdings Limited Partnership
120 Broadway, New York, NY 10271
firstsecondbooks.com
mackids.com

Text © 2022 by Clint McElroy
Illustrations © 2022 by Eliza Kinkz
All rights reserved

Library of Congress Cataloging-in-Publication Data is available.

Our books may be purchased in bulk for promotional, educational, or business use.
Please contact your local bookseller or the Macmillan Corporate
and Premium Sales Department at (800) 221-7945 ext. 5442
or by email at MacmillanSpecialMarkets@macmillan.com.

FIRST
EDITION

First edition, 2022
Edited by Calista Brill and Kiara Valdez
Cover design by Kirk Benshoff
Interior book design by Kirk Benshoff

Printed in China by 1010 Printing International Limited, North Point, Hong Kong

ISBN 978-1-250-24932-6
1  3  5  7  9  10  8  6  4  2

Don't miss your next favorite book from First Second! For the latest updates go to
firstsecondnewsletter.com and sign up for our enewsletter.

BY ART
WE LIVE

#1 Grand-Kid

So you've decided to be a grandchild.

That means you have to take on the important job of handling . . .

It's a big responsibility, but with the right care and treatment . . .

Any coupons?

. . . you will find that grandparents can be loyal and loving companions.

Playtime is very important
to grandparents. Especially
games where they have to use
their imaginations.

When it comes to toys, keep it simple.
If a toy is too complicated, your grandparent
will become discouraged and say something like,
"Toys were a lot better when I was your age."

And NO video games.
It's just too much for them.

Also, they seem to enjoy playing games that let them sit in chairs.

Grandparents need to be monitored closely,
especially when it comes to "restroom
activities," if you know what I mean.

I don't know why, but it's like they are OBSESSED with going to the potty!

Grumble
Rumble

The feeding of grandparents is simple.

This can work to your advantage because . . .

Of course it's also important that your grandparent gets plenty of exercise.

Dancing can be a good activity for them.

They are especially fond of dance moves like the Bump, the Hustle, and the Funky Chicken.

It can be fun to let them do tricks with you.
Like pulling a quarter out of your ear . . .

. . . burping on command . . .

. . . and one that involves pulling a finger,
but I'll let you find out about that one on your own.

After a long day of building forts, eating triple sundaes, and dancing the Funky Chicken, it will be easy to get your grandparent to go down for bedtime.

Get them to sit with you in a rocking chair.
If you can get them to sing to you, even better.
("Rainbow Connection" is a personal favorite.)

Soon, you'll have them sleeping like a baby.

CONTRA COSTA COUNTY LIBRARY

31901068128356